Kelly's heart thumped with exci[tement] as she walked round the circle of Kitty [Kabins.] frosted glass doors were cats of all breeds, shapes and sizes, and they all needed to find someone to love them! Kelly wished she could take every one of them home with her. However was she going to choose? A Siamese cat sitting on a cushion stared regally at her as she peeped in, and a pair of black and white cats, curled up together on a platform, twitched their paws in their sleep. Then, suddenly, out of the corner of her eye, Kelly noticed something small and white dashing madly around the Kitty Kabin she had just walked past.

Kelly took a step back and peered inside the Kabin.

"Awww!" she gasped. The cutest kitten she had ever seen was pressing its dusky pink nose against the glass that separated them. Kelly crouched down and put her finger on the glass.

"Hello little kitten," she whispered.

"Miaow!" The little ball of fluff patted at the glass with tiny pink paw pads – and Kelly fell head over heels in love.

Have you read all these books in the **Battersea Dogs & Cats Home** series?

BAILEY'S story

CHESTER'S story

RUSTY'S story

MAX'S story

DAISY'S story

SNOWY'S story

MISTY'S story

COSMO'S story

STELLA'S story

ANGEL'S story

❖ ❖ ❖ ❖

ANGEL'S
story

by
Jane Clarke

Illustrated by Artful Doodlers
Puzzle illustrations by Jason Chapman

RED FOX

BATTERSEA DOGS & CATS HOME: ANGEL'S STORY
A RED FOX BOOK 978 1 849 414110 4

First published in Great Britain by Red Fox,
an imprint of Random House Children's Publishers UK
A Random House Group Company

This edition published 2011

3 5 7 9 10 8 6 4 2

Set in 13/20 Stone Informal

Red Fox Books are published by Random House Children's Publishers UK,
61–63 Uxbridge Road, London W5 5SA

www.**randomhousechildrens**.co.uk
www.randomhouse.co.uk

Addresses for companies within The Random House Group Limited
can be found at: www.randomhouse.co.uk/offices.htm

THE RANDOM HOUSE GROUP Limited Reg. No. 954009

A CIP catalogue record for this book is available from the British Library.

The Random House Group Limited supports The Forest Stewardship
Council® (FSC®), the leading international forest-certification organisation.
Our books carrying the FSC label are printed on FSC®-certified paper.
FSC is the only forest-certification scheme supported by the leading
environmental organisations, including Greenpeace. Our
paper procurement policy can be found at
www.randomhouse.co.uk/environment

MIX
Paper from
responsible sources
FSC
FSC® C016897

Printed and bound in Great Britain by Clays Ltd, St Ives PLC

Meet the stars of the
Battersea Dogs & Cats
Home series to date . . .

Turn to page **93** for lots
of information on the
Battersea Dogs & Cats Home,
plus some cool activities!

🐾 🐾 🐾 🐾

Meet the stars of the Battersea Dogs & Cats Home series to date . . .

Bailey

Misty

Chester

Rusty

Max

Daisy

Snowy

Stella

Huey

Cosmo

Angel

Angel in a Kitty Kabin

Kelly Chambers gazed adoringly into the cat carrier on the car seat beside her. A tiny white kitten with long whiskers, a dusky pink nose and big blue eyes gazed innocently back at her.

"Angel, you are the cutest kitten in the whole wide world!" Kelly murmured.

She could hardly believe she was on her way home with her very own kitten!

Ever since she'd learned to talk, she'd been trying to convince her mum, dad and big brother Felix to let her have one. Kelly was so happy that they'd finally agreed! She playfully wriggled the end of her woolly scarf in front of the cat carrier. Angel pricked her ears, then poked a tiny paw through the wire and patted at Kelly's scarf.

Kelly smiled lovingly at her adorable kitten. She couldn't wait to get home and introduce Angel to Joey!

Joey was the old Border collie who had been with their family since before Kelly was born. Kelly loved Joey lots, but Joey was Felix's dog – Angel would curl on *her* lap, and love *her* best! For the longest time, Mum and Dad had said it wouldn't be fair on Joey – or a kitten – to have to live with each other because dogs and cats found it hard to get along. But when they'd gone camping in France, Joey had stayed with

Grandma and
her old tabby
cat, Patches.
Joey and
Patches had
become
such friends
that when
they'd gone
to collect
Joey, they
found him
snuggled up with
Patches on Grandma's best mat!

"Look at that!" Felix had said, "Joey
loves that cat!"

Kelly's mum and dad had suggested
that they find Joey a kitten friend from
Battersea Dogs & Cats Home, because ten
years ago, Joey had been a rescue dog

from the same Home. Kelly had danced
around hugging everyone, shouting
"Yay!" at the top of her voice and Joey
had joined in, barking excitedly!

Two weeks ago, the whole family had
made an appointment to visit the cattery
at Battersea Dogs & Cats Home.

"We already have an old dog called Joey," Kelly had told the nice man, whose name was Woody.

Woody nodded. "So you're looking for a companion cat . . ."

"A kitten!" Kelly corrected him excitedly.

Woody smiled. "I'm sure we can find a confident young kitten that will be happy to live with Joey and your family," he said. "Follow me . . ."

He led them up the spiral stairs into Battersea's new state-of-the-art cattery.

Kelly's heart thumped with excitement as she walked round the circle of Kitty Kabins. Behind the frosted glass doors were cats of all breeds, shapes and sizes, and they all needed to find someone to love them! Kelly wished she could take every one of them home with her. However was she going to choose? A Siamese cat sitting on a cushion stared regally at her as she peeped in, and a pair of black and white cats, curled up together on a platform, twitched their paws in their sleep.

Then, suddenly, out of the corner of her
eye, Kelly noticed something small and
white dashing madly around the Kitty
Kabin she had just walked past.

Kelly took a step back and peered
inside the Kabin.

"Awww!" she gasped. The cutest kitten
she had ever seen was pressing its dusky
pink nose against the glass that
separated them. Kelly crouched down
and put her finger
on the glass.

"Hello little kitten,"
she whispered.

"Miaow!" The
little ball of fluff
patted at the
glass with tiny
pink paw pads –
and Kelly fell
head over heels
in love.

"I've found my
kitten!" she announced
to her family.

"She's called Angel," Woody told them.

"Angel!" Kelly squeaked in delight.
"That's a perfect name!"

"Angel's one of our newest recruits to
Battersea," Woody went on. "But don't let
her name fool you. She can be trouble!
Would you like to go in and meet her?"

"Yes, *please!*" Kelly leapt excitedly to her feet as Woody opened the pen and let the Chambers family step inside. Angel rushed forward to greet Kelly, pushing her silky head against Kelly's out-stretched hand to say hello.

"Well, she's definitely not shy!" Dad laughed, as Angel strutted up to him and wound herself round his legs, her tiny tail waving confidently in the air.

"She should get on fine with everyone," Felix agreed. "I think Joey will love her!"

"We'll send someone round to meet Joey and check that your house is suitable," Woody told them. "If all goes well, you can come and collect Angel after that . . ."

A cheeky *miaow* jolted Kelly back to the present. Her scarf had slipped off the car seat and Angel was looking for something to play with!

Kelly laughed. "That's Angel's way of saying she's waited long enough, and it's time to play in her new home!" she said, as Dad parked the car in front of their house.

Angel Explores

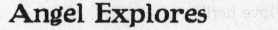

Kelly hopped impatiently from foot to foot as Dad carefully picked up the cat carrier from the back seat and opened the front door.

"We're home!" Kelly yelled, feeling as if she'd burst with excitement. Mum and Felix gathered in the kitchen doorway with Joey and watched Dad place the cat carrier on the hall floor. The old dog sniffed the air as Kelly knelt down to open the wire door.

"We should stand back," Mum whispered. "We don't want to scare her. It may take a while for such a little kitten to get used to her new surroundings and come out . . ."

There was an excited *miaow* and a flash of white fur as Angel darted straight at Joey and tried to pounce on the end of his tail.

That's my brave kitten! Kelly thought proudly.

Joey backed away with a startled *woof!*

"It's OK, boy, she won't hurt you," Kelly reassured him.

Joey's tail wagged uncertainly. Angel danced on her hind legs as she tried to catch it with her paws. Before Kelly could stop her, she'd grabbed hold of Joey's tail and was dangling from it!

Grrr! Joey growled quietly.

Kelly quickly scooped Angel into her arms in case Joey decided to nip. Joey had never bitten anyone or anything, but then again, he had never had a tiny kitten swing from his tail before!

"It's all a bit of a shock for Joey," Felix said. "I'll take him out for a walk." He clipped Joey's lead onto his collar.

"Good idea," Mum agreed. "That will give Angel a chance to explore and settle in. Kelly, show Angel her litter box in case she needs it."

Kelly wrinkled her nose, but house-
training was part of the
deal, so she gently
placed Angel in the
new litter box in
the utility room.
Angel jumped
straight out again
and scampered into
the kitchen, where she
tried out her paws on the
scratching post next to the brand new
kitty basket.

"At least you know
what that's for,"
Kelly giggled as she
watched Angel
climb up the post.
Her kitten was
having such fun!

Angel dropped down from the post and shot off into the living room like a little white whirlwind.

Kelly raced after her, just in time to see Angel spring onto Mum's new sofa and claw herself up the cushions onto the backrest.

"Don't let Mum catch you doing that!"

Kelly whispered with a smile as Angel tightrope-walked along the back of the sofa. She picked up her fluffy little kitten and carried her to the bottom of the stairs. Angel wriggled excitedly in her arms.

"Come and see my room," Kelly said, setting her down. "You'll love it!"

Angel looked up at the stairs. Each steep step was higher than she was. *It must be like a cliff to her*, Kelly thought, stopping halfway up the stairs to watch.

Angel stretched her front paws onto the first step and scrabbled with her back feet.

"That's it!" Kelly encouraged Angel as she pulled herself up the first step. "Yay! You did it!"

Angel managed the second stair even faster, and by the third step, she was bouncing up the stairs like she was on springs.

"You're so clever!" Kelly told her. Angel sat on the landing at the top of the stairs and looked up at Kelly.

Miaow? she mewed. She looked soooo sweet! Kelly picked her up and cradled her in her arms.

"This is the bathroom, and Mum and Dad's bedroom, and Felix's bedroom – don't go in there . . . " Kelly showed Angel the closed doors. "But here's my bedroom, and you're very, very welcome!"

She set Angel down on her bed. The little kitten glanced curiously around her and began to pounce on the flower patterns on Kelly's duvet. It was the cutest thing Kelly had ever seen!

Kelly grinned from ear to ear as Angel did an extra-high pounce, tumbled off the bed and scampered back out onto the landing.

Miaow? Angel stood mewing outside the cupboard next to the bathroom. The tip of her tail swished.

"That's the airing cupboard," Kelly told her.

Warm air wafted out of the cupboard as Kelly opened the door to show Angel the shelves of towels and bed sheets, and the rail where Mum hung damp washing to dry.

Angel stretched her head towards the airing cupboard. Kelly could see her long white whiskers twitching as they sensed the warmth.

"Let's go back down, I've got lots of things to show you before Joey gets back." Kelly pushed the cupboard door closed, gathered up Angel, and carried her back downstairs and into the kitchen where Mum was preparing dinner.

"This is your new bed. I chose it!" Kelly told Angel, placing her in the soft kitty basket. But Angel jumped straight back out and scampered over to Joey's bed on the opposite side of the kitchen! Kelly watched Angel's whiskers twitch as she ran her pink nose over the dog basket. Then she stood in the middle of it and began treading and kneading it with her paws. Contented purrs echoed round the kitchen as the kitten curled up in the old dog's bed. Kelly thought she'd never seen anything so adorable in her life!

"I don't know what Joey will make of Angel sleeping in his bed!" Mum laughed.

Kelly sat down beside Angel and scratched the kitten under her chin. Angel stretched out her neck then tilted her head, so that Kelly could stroke the soft fur behind her tiny ears. The kitten's eyes half-closed with pleasure and she purred louder and louder.

"Well, I think you're just perfect!" Kelly told Angel. "And Joey will love you, too, won't he?"

They were about to find out! Angel
opened an eye as the kitchen door
opened. Felix and Joey were back from
their walk . . .

Angel Makes Herself
at Home

Joey stood in the kitchen doorway
looking in disbelief at the little white
kitten in his bed.

Woof! he barked indignantly. *Woof!*
Woof!

Angel opened her eyes wide and gave
a surprised *mew*. She looked ever so tiny
compared with the big dog. Kelly scooped

her up as Joey came over. He sniffed
suspiciously at his bed, then looked up
questioningly at Kelly.

"Good boy, Joey," Kelly reassured him.
Joey's tail twitched uncertainly.

Kelly knelt down,
holding Angel in her
arms so that Joey
could sniff the
kitten's head.

"Joey, meet
Angel. You're
going to be great
friends," Kelly told the
puzzled-looking dog.

Miaow! Angel pushed
her nose towards Joey. Kelly
smiled at the little kitten's attempt to
make friends. Joey's tail started to wag
slowly as he sized up the tiny ball of fur.

Suddenly, Angel put out
a tiny paw and
playfully tapped
the old dog on his
greying muzzle.
Joey's lip curled.
Grrr! Joey
growled quietly.

Kelly leapt to her
feet, holding Angel out
of Joey's reach in case the big dog decided
to snap at her kitten. But Joey had gone
into a sulk.

The elderly collie
flopped down
grumpily onto his
bed and turned
his back on
everyone. He gave
a deep growly sigh.

"You should keep Angel out of Joey's bed," Felix told Kelly. "It isn't fair to make him share at his age."

"Perhaps it would be best if we don't leave them in the kitchen together just yet," Mum said thoughtfully. "Angel can sleep in the living room until Joey has got to know her properly." She gathered up Angel's scratching post and kitty basket and took them into the next room.

"I'll look after Angel," Kelly said protectively as she carried her kitten out of the kitchen.

"Don't let her damage the furniture," Mum warned as she shut the door behind them.

"I won't!" Kelly set up Angel's things in the corner of the living room. "Playtime, Angel. Look!" Kelly took a table-tennis ball out of the kitten's bed and rolled it across the floor. Angel flicked the tip of her tail, scampered after the ball, and pounced. The smooth ball shot out of her paws. Angel caught it mid air and rolled over and over with it, showing her pink tummy under her downy white fur.

"Awww!" Kelly murmured. Angel was like the cutest, prettiest, picture-book-kitten ever! She watched happily as Angel tumbled and pounced after the ball until it rolled under the sofa and the little kitten stretched her paws out to find it.

Her tail twitched as she wriggled out backwards, dragging the end of a piece of wool that had caught on one of claws. The wool lay like a thin worm on the carpet.

Angel pricked her ears and watched it closely. Then, suddenly, she pounced on it, grabbed it in her mouth and pulled. A long length of yarn seemed to free itself from beneath the sofa and slither across the carpet. Angel twitched her ears and pounced on it again.

It looked like Mum's new sofa was coming apart!

Mum's going to kill us! Kelly thought. She stuck her hand under the sofa and grabbed something soft and squashy. Phew! It was a little ball of powder-blue wool – not part of the sofa at all!

Miaow! Angel leapt on the ball of wool, and patted it from paw to paw. Kelly giggled as her naughty little kitten grabbed the end in her mouth and scampered excitedly round the room with it. Kelly took hold of one end of the wool and slowly dragged it across the carpet. Angel stalked it and pounced, again and again. It was so much fun to play with her kitten! Angel was in kitty heaven, and so was Kelly.

Suddenly there was a gasp from the door. Kelly and Angel both froze in the tangle of unravelled wool.

"What are you doing? That's my knitting wool!" Mum spluttered. "Kelly, your new kitten is a bundle of trouble!" she scolded.

Kelly's heart sank. What would she do if Mum said Angel had to go back to the cattery?

Learning to Share

Angel looked up at Kelly's mum with her bright blue eyes open wide.

Miaow! she mewed softly, tilting her head to one side.

Mum's eyes began to crinkle as she looked at the wool-wrapped kitten.

"Oh, it's impossible to be cross with you for long," she said. "You're too sweet!" She smiled as she stroked Angel behind the ears.

Kelly breathed a sigh of relief.

"But you have to learn what things are yours and what things belong to other people," Mum told the little kitten. She looked meaningfully at Kelly.

"It wasn't Angel's fault!" Kelly said, as she untangled Angel from the wool. "It was my idea to play with the wool. Angel's very clever, so she'll soon learn what things are hers."

Kelly smiled confidently at Mum. "Dinner time is a good place to start. I can teach Angel what's her food, and what's Joey's."

"I'm not sure Joey and Angel should try and eat together in the same room just yet," Mum said, winding the wool back into a ball.

"They'll be fine," Kelly said, with more confidence than she felt. She carried Angel into the kitchen. Joey was fast asleep and snoring in his basket. Mum handed Kelly a small dish of dried kitten food, and Felix a big dish of dry dog food.

"Dinner time," Kelly and Felix said together, putting down their pets' bowls at the opposite ends of the kitchen.

"This is yours, Angel." Kelly set her kitten down next to her bowl. Angel took one sniff at the kitten food, then bounded across the room to Joey's bowl which Felix had put down next to Joey's bed.

Kelly watched open-mouthed as Angel stuck her nose into the doggy nibbles and began crunching. Joey looked up groggily from his deep sleep.

Woof! he barked indignantly. *Woof! WOOF!*

Angel's fur puffed up all over her tiny body and she bristled from nose to tail. She looked twice her normal size. Joey stared at her in shock as she dashed back to her bowl and began to wolf down her own dinner.

Kelly couldn't help laughing at her cheeky kitten, but Felix was frowning. Joey had tucked his tail between his legs and was gobbling down his dinner as fast as he could.

"I told you to keep your kitten away from Joey's things," Felix told Kelly. "You wouldn't like it if Joey ate Angel's food, would you?" Kelly had to admit she wouldn't.

***

After everyone had finished
dinner that evening,
Joey settled back
down in his
basket. Kelly
took Angel to
the litter box,
then carried her
into the living
room, being careful to close

the kitchen
door behind
her.
"Time for
bed," she
told Angel,
placing her
in the comfy
kitty basket.

Angel sat in the basket and
stretched out her back
legs. Kelly watched,
entranced, as the
kitten carefully licked
each leg in turn and
her fluffy tummy with
her sandpapery pink
tongue. She had to twist her head right
round to wash her back. Last of all, Angel
licked her front paw, and
rubbed it first behind
one ear, and then the
other. Then, purring
happily, she curled
up and went to sleep.
    Kelly looked
lovingly down at Angel.

    "Felix and Joey aren't used to having a
kitten around the place," she murmured.

"But I think you're really, really sweet, and I'm very happy that you're here."

Kelly kissed Angel gently on top of her head and went up to bed. Felix and Joey hadn't got along with her kitten as well as she'd hoped, but they'd come round soon, wouldn't they? Kelly was too tired to lie awake worrying. It had been such an exciting, busy day she was too tired even to dream!

In a Tangle

On Monday morning, Kelly got up early so she could spend some time with Angel before she went off to school. While Mum and Felix were busy crunching their cornflakes, the mischievous little kitten crept into the kitchen, jumped onto the windowsill, and started tapping at Mum's spider plant with her tiny paw. Kelly held her breath, expecting someone

to complain, but Angel looked so cute
that even Felix started smiling at her
antics. Then Dad walked into the kitchen
holding up a pair of his work
shoes.

"My laces are all
tangled up," he
said in a
puzzled voice.
"It's very
odd. They
weren't like
this when I
put them
away on
Friday."

Kelly glanced at the
door between the living
room and the kitchen. When she'd come
downstairs that morning, she had been a

bit worried to find that it was open, along with the door from the living room into the hall. But Angel had been fast asleep in her basket – and Joey was still fast asleep in his.

"Where did you leave your shoes?" she asked her dad.

"In the cupboard under the stairs," Dad said. "I noticed the door was open a crack . . ."

"My football boots are in there too!" Felix dashed into the hall and returned clutching a tangle of football boots and trainers. The laces were all knotted up and wound round each other.

"I've got football after school," Felix groaned, as he tried to undo the knots. "This is your kitten's fault," he told Kelly.

"Maybe it was Joey," Kelly said. "He likes shoes." She didn't sound very convincing, even to herself.

"Joey hasn't chewed up anything since he was a puppy," Felix retorted. "But we all saw what Angel did to Mum's knitting wool. There's the culprit." He pointed to the kitchen windowsill.

Angel was getting more and more excited as the leaves on the spider plant wobbled. She rolled on her back underneath the plant, trying to catch the leaves with all four of her paws. Kelly couldn't help giggling.

Mum and Dad began to laugh too, but Felix wasn't amused.

"I haven't got time to untangle my football boots and walk Joey before school," he grumbled. "That kitten is nothing but trouble!" He didn't even laugh when Angel tapped a leaf so hard that she lost her balance and fell off the windowsill into the empty sink with a surprised mew.

Joey woke up and began to bark.

"Come on, Joey," Felix said, dumping his football boots by the back door and clipping on Joey's lead. "Let's get out of here!" Felix slammed the back door behind him.

Kelly stopped
laughing.

"Felix and
Joey don't like
Angel!" she
said, feeling the
tears come into
her eyes as she
scooped her damp
kitten out of the sink.

"You have to be patient," Dad told her.

"Joey and Felix just
need a bit of
time to get
used to
having
another
animal
around the
house."

"I hope so," Kelly sniffed. She gave Angel a big hug as she carried her into the living room. The little cat mewed softly as Kelly put her in her basket with her toys.

"Try to be good while I'm at school," she whispered.

Angel in Trouble

"I'm home, where's Angel?"

Kelly rushed in through the front door and threw her coat and backpack on the floor. She'd spent all day at school wondering how things were going at home.

"Angel's fine! She's asleep in the living room," Mum called from the kitchen. "I came into the kitchen to make the tea

and shut the door so that Joey could have
a nap. He's been out in the garden all
day."

Kelly raced into the living room. Her
tummy did a flip.
Angel's basket
was empty!
Kelly looked
round the
room,
peering under
the furniture,
but there was
no sign of the
furry white kitten.
She dashed upstairs and poked her head
into all the rooms. Then she clattered
back down and burst into the kitchen.

"I can't find Angel," she said in a
panic.

"She's got to be in the house somewhere," Mum reassured her. "Kittens aren't allowed outside, so I made sure all the windows were shut."

Kelly and Mum looked high and low, but they couldn't find Angel anywhere. By the time Dad got home from work, Kelly's tummy felt as if it was full of frogs doing somersaults, and her voice was all choked up when she told him what had happened.

"Try not to worry, love," Dad told her. "Angel will turn up. Have you checked Joey's bed?" he joked.

But Kelly was
desperate and
any idea was
better than
nothing! She
hurried into
the kitchen
and felt all
round Joey.
The old dog
woke up and
sleepily wagged his tail.

"Angel's not here!" Kelly wailed.
"She'll be lonely and frightened on her
own!"

"I'll help you look for Angel. Just give
me five minutes to change," Dad
promised her, heading upstairs.

"Your clean jeans are in the airing
cupboard," Mum called up after him.

There was a sudden yell from upstairs.
Aarrrgh!

Mum and Kelly leapt up the stairs to
see Dad standing on the landing
clutching Angel in his arms!

Kelly's heart jumped for joy.

"She found a nice warm place to sleep
– in the airing cupboard,"
Dad laughed,
stroking Angel's
fur. "She
jumped out
when I opened
the door and
scared the
living
daylights out
of me!" He
handed the
kitten to Kelly.

"I was so worried about you, Angel," Kelly murmured affectionately as she cuddled her naughty kitten. Angel purred happily.

There was a loud *woof!* from outside the back door, followed by a creak as the door opened, and a clang as it was slammed shut.

"Where is everyone?" Felix yelled.

Mum, Dad, Kelly and Angel headed down to the kitchen. Felix was on his knees stroking Joey's ears.

"You left Joey outside all on his own!" Felix said accusingly. "You only care about that silly kitten."

"That's not true," Mum said. "I've
been checking on Joey all day. Angel got
lost and we were looking for her, that's
all. Now, how was your football
practice?"

"I didn't get to play! I had to watch
because I left my boots at home!"

Kelly glanced towards the back door.
Felix's boots were lying where he had
thrown them that morning.

Felix pointed at
the little kitten
with a finger
that was
quivering
with rage.
Kelly
clutched
Angel tightly
to her chest.

"It's all Angel's fault! I wish she'd never come to live with us!" Felix thundered. "Everything was fine when we just had Joey!"

Woof! Joey barked. *Woof! Woof! Woof!*

Kelly retreated with Angel into the living room. Through the door, she could hear Felix shouting and Joey barking. Mum was telling Felix not to shout because it wound up the dog.

". . . Joey and Angel will learn to get along together, it's just taking a bit longer than we thought it would, that's all . . ." Mum said. "You must try to be kinder to Kelly and her kitten."

Kelly stopped listening with a sigh. She put down Angel and retrieved her school backpack.

"My best friend, Cheryl, gave me a present to give to you," she told Angel. She rummaged in her backpack and took out a little fish-shaped pouch.

"It's got catnip inside. Cheryl's cat loves catnip, so I think you'll like it too!" Kelly rolled the toy across the floor towards Angel.

Angel pounced on it gleefully and rolled over, grabbing at the catnip fish with all four of her tiny paws. Kelly smiled fondly at her adorable pet as she tumbled over and over with her new toy.

But she couldn't help worrying. Would Angel ever be able to share a room with Joey?

How could she stop Felix being so
unreasonable? There just had to be a way
for them to get along.

A Big Scare

Things didn't improve much the next week, though Felix did calm down enough to apologize to Kelly for what he had said.

"Angel's very cute, really," he admitted.

But Joey clearly didn't feel the same. Most of the time, he kept out of Angel's way, but on Sunday morning, Angel took

a drink out of Joey's water bowl and Joey
chased her out of the kitchen,
barking loudly!

"I'll
take Angel
up to my
bedroom and keep
her out of Joey's way,"
Kelly told everyone. "I've got
some homework to catch up on."

Kelly didn't usually have homework to do on Sunday morning, but she'd got behind with her homework during the week as she'd been spending so much time with her new kitten. It was fun having Angel sit on her desk in her room and keep her company. The trouble was, Angel liked to lie on Kelly's papers like a furry white paperweight, or join in with Kelly's homework like it was a game!

"Now, Angel. I have to choose a dinosaur, draw it and write about it." Kelly took a dinosaur book out of her backpack and put it on her desk.

"Which dino do you think I should do?" Kelly asked her kitten as she turned the pages of the book. Angel patted at the corners of the pages. Then, when the book was open at the picture of a fierce meat-eater, Angel pounced on the picture.

"T-Rex. Good choice," Kelly giggled as she got out her notebook and pencil box and began to draw. Angel pounced on the end of her pencil as she drew. It was great fun! Kelly gave up drawing and swished her pencil so that Angel could skitter across the desk chasing it.

Mum stuck her head round the door.

"I don't think Angel is helping you concentrate!" she laughed. "I'll take her downstairs."

"Can't she sit on my bed?" Kelly pleaded. "I can get on then."

"That didn't work last week, did it?" Mum reminded Kelly. "Get your homework out of the way, then you'll have plenty of time to play with Angel after dinner – it's your favourite, roast chicken. I've just taken it out of the oven, so you only have half an hour before I dish up."

"Ok, Mum," Kelly said reluctantly. She gave Angel a stroke and handed her to Mum to take downstairs.

Things went much faster without Angel's help! Kelly was just about finished when there was a thunderous *crash!* from the kitchen. Kelly jumped in surprise. What was that? To her horror, the noise was followed by a shrill miaow and a volley of excited barks.

"No!" Mum yelled at the top of her voice.

Kelly's heart pounded as she raced downstairs.

Angel must have got into the kitchen
with Joey. It sounded like something
terrible had happened!

Puurrfect Friends

Kelly raced downstairs, ready to rescue her poor little kitten.

Mum, Dad and Felix were standing at the kitchen door. Mum was smiling, Dad was chuckling, and Felix was laughing so hard he could hardly stand!

"What's going on?" Kelly pushed her way to the front. "Is Angel OK?"

Mum's roast chicken tray was lying

where it had crashed to the kitchen floor.
The roast chicken had rolled into Angel's
corner of the kitchen – and Angel and
Joey were standing side by side, tucking
into the juicy meal.

"Angel! Joey!" Kelly
gasped. The two
naughty animals
paused. Joey wagged
his tail cheekily. Then
they both plunged back
into their meal.

Kelly's mouth dropped open.

"Joey's realized that having a cat
around can have its benefits," Felix
gasped gleefully.

"Angel must have jumped up onto the
kitchen counter and knocked off the
roasting tray," Dad explained with a
grin. "What a feast for both of them!"

"Looks like it's pizza for Sunday dinner, I'm afraid," Mum sighed, but even she couldn't help smiling.

"I don't care what we eat!" Kelly exclaimed. "I'm just happy that Angel and Joey have found a way to be friends!"

"We'd better stop them before they make themselves sick," said Felix, dragging Joey away from the chicken.

Mum scooped up
the remains in
the roasting pan.

Kelly picked
up her sticky
kitten. Angel's
pure-white fur
was speckled with
brown gravy. She
blew her an air kiss on

the top of her head.
"What a
clever way to
get Joey to
like you!"
she
whispered.
Woof? Joey
barked politely
up at Kelly.

Kelly bent down and put Angel on the
floor in front of him. She held her breath
as Joey stretched out his grey muzzle and
gently touched Angel's
dusky pink nose
with his.

Then the old dog affectionately licked the gravy off the little white kitten, all the while wagging his tail.

Miaow, Angel mewed contentedly and began to purr.

"Awww!" Felix said. "Joey loves that kitten!" Kelly could hardly believe her ears!

Mum and Dad gathered round Kelly, Felix and the two new best pet friends.

Kelly grinned happily at everyone's smiling faces as the kitchen filled with purrs. Angel might not always behave like an angel, but her cute little kitten was really part of the Chambers family now!

Read on for lots more . . .

🐾 🐾 🐾 🐾

Battersea Dogs & Cats Home

Battersea Dogs & Cats Home is a charity that aims never to turn away a dog or cat in need of our help. We reunite lost dogs and cats with their owners; when we can't do this, we care for them until new homes can be found for them; and we educate the public about responsible pet ownership. Every year the Home takes in over 10,000 dogs and cats. In addition to the site in south-west London, the Home also has two other centres based at Old Windsor, Berkshire, and Brands Hatch, Kent.

The original site in Holloway

History

The Temporary Home for Lost and Starving Dogs was originally opened in a stable yard in Holloway in 1860 by Mary Tealby after she found a starving puppy in the street. There was no one to look after him, so she took him home and nursed him back to health. She was so worried about the other dogs wandering the streets that she opened the Temporary Home for Lost and Starving Dogs. The Home was established to help to look after them all and find them new homes.

Sadly Mary Tealby died in 1865, aged sixty-four, and little more is known about her, but her good work was continued. In 1871 the Home moved to its present site in Battersea, and was renamed the Dogs' Home Battersea.

Some important dates for the Home:

1883 – Battersea start taking in cats.

1914 – 100 sledge dogs are housed at the Hackbridge site, in preparation for Ernest Shackleton's second Antarctic expedition.

1956 – Queen Elizabeth II becomes patron of the Home.

2004 – Red the Lurcher's night-time antics become world famous when he is caught on camera regularly escaping from his kennel and liberating his canine chums for midnight feasts.

2007 – The BBC broadcast *Animal Rescue Live* from the Home for three weeks from mid-July to early August.

Fun and Learning

Amy Watson has been working at
Battersea Dogs & Cats Home for six years
and has been the Home's Education
Officer for two and a half years. Amy's
role means that she organizes all the
school visits to the Home for children
aged sixteen and under, and regularly
visits schools around Battersea's three

sites to teach children how to behave and stay safe around dogs and cats, and all about responsible dog and cat ownership. She also regularly features on the Battersea website – www.battersea.org.uk – giving tips and advice on how to train your dog or cat under the "Amy's Answers" section.

On most school visits Amy can take a dog with her, so she is normally accompanied by her beautiful ex-Battersea dog Hattie. Hattie has been living with Amy for just over a year and really enjoys meeting new children and helping Amy with her work.

The process for re-homing a dog or a cat

When a lost dog or cat arrives, Battersea's Lost Dogs & Cats Line works hard to try to find the animal's owners. If, after seven days, they have not been able to reunite them, the search for a new home can begin.

The Home works hard to find caring, permanent new homes for all the lost and unwanted dogs and cats.

Dogs and cats have their own characters and so staff at the Home will spend time getting to know every dog and cat. This helps decide the type of home the dog or cat needs.

There are five stages of the re-homing process at Battersea Dogs & Cats Home. Battersea's re-homing team wants to find you the perfect pet, sometimes this can take a while, so please be patient while we search for your new friend!

1 Application

2 Interview

3 Home visit

4 Searching for a pet

5 Leaving with your new pet

Have a look at our website:
http://www.battersea.org.uk/dogs/ rehoming/index.html for more details!

"Did you know?" questions about dogs and cats

- Puppies do not open their eyes until they are about two weeks old.

- According to *The Guinness Book of Records*, the smallest living dog is a long-haired Chihuahua called Danka Kordak from Slovakia, who is 13.8cm tall and 18.8cm long.

- Dalmatians, with all those cute black spots, are actually born white.

- The greyhound is the fastest dog on earth. They can reach speeds of up to 45 miles per hour.

- The first living creature sent into space was a female dog named Laika.

- Cats spend 15% of their day grooming themselves and a massive 70% of their day sleeping.

- Cats see six times better in the dark than we do.

- A cat's tail helps it to balance when it is on the move – especially when it is jumping.

- The cat, giraffe and camel are the only animals that walk by moving both their left feet, then both their right feet, when walking.

Dos and Don'ts of looking after dogs and cats

Dogs dos and don'ts

DO

- Be gentle and quiet around dogs at all times – treat them how you would like to be treated.

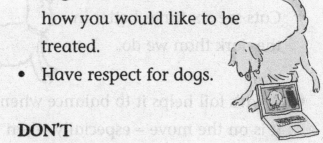

- Have respect for dogs.

DON'T

- Sneak up on a dog – you could scare them.
- Tease a dog – it's not fair.
- Stare at a dog – dogs can find this scary.
- Disturb a dog who is sleeping or eating.

- Assume a dog wants to play with you. Just like you, sometimes they may want to be left alone.
- Approach a dog who is without an owner as you won't know if the dog is friendly or not.

Cats dos and don'ts

DO
- Be gentle and quiet around cats at all times.
- Have respect for cats.
- Let a cat approach you in their own time.

DON'T
- Never stare at a cat as they can find this intimidating.

- Tease a cat – it's not fair.
- Disturb a sleeping or eating cat – they may not want attention or to play.
- Assume a cat will always want to play. Like you, sometimes they want to be left alone.

WELCOME

Here is a delicious recipe for you to follow.

Remember to ask an adult to help you.

Cheddar Cheese Cat Cookies

You will need:

227g grated Cheddar cheese

(use at room temperature)

114g margarine

1 egg

1 clove of garlic (crushed)

172g wholewheat flour

30g wheatgerm

1 teaspoon salt

30ml milk

Preheat the oven to 375°F/190°C/gas mark 5.

Cream the cheese and margarine together. When smooth, add the egg and garlic and mix well. Add the flour, wheatgerm and salt. Mix well until a dough forms. Add the milk and mix again.

Chill the mixture in the fridge for one hour.

Roll the dough onto a floured surface until it is about 4cm thick. Use cookie cutters to cut out shapes.

Bake on an ungreased baking tray for 15–18 minutes.

Cool to room temperature and store in an airtight container in the fridge.

Some fun pet-themed puzzles!

What a cat needs!

Here is a list of things that a cat needs for a long, happy and healthy life. See if you can find them in the word search and while you look, think why they might be so important. The words could be written backwards, diagonally, forwards, up and down so look carefully and GOOD LUCK!

FOOD
SCRATCHING POST
WATER
MICROCHIP
LITTER TRAY
TREATS
COLLAR
TOYS
TAG
PLAY
BED
VET CARE
LOVE
GROOMING
RESPONSIBLE OWNERS

Remember: a cat needs the litter in its tray change at least once a day.

Can you think of any other things a cat may need? Write them in the spaces below.

Cat Breeds Crossword

Across

1 These orange and black coloured cats are nearly always female. (13)

3 These spotted cats are the result of breeding with wild cats and share their name with a type of tiger. (6)

4 Brown cat with black stripes. (5)

7 A blue eyed oriental cat with a white body and colour on its head and tail. (7)

9 Like the siamese but all one colour and shares its name with people who come from Burma . (7)

10 This colour of cat can be deaf and may need sun cream on its ears on hot days. (5)

11 This breed of cat has no tail and comes from the Isle of Man. (4)

12 A type of persian that shares its name with a pet rodent with thick fur. (10)

13 This breed has no fur at all and shares its name with a statue in Egypt. (6)

Down

2 This cat is always trying to catch Tweety Pie. (9)

4 This cat is always getting beaten up by a mouse called Jerry. (3)

5 These grey coloured cats have thick fur and come from England. (7,4)

6 The name of the Blue Peter cat. (6)

8 A long haired breed that needs lots of grooming. (7)

9 The colour of cats that witches have and at Battersea they often find it harder to get homes because of their colour. (5)

Transform these white cats by adding some colour. You could turn them into one of the breeds from the crossword or make them look like your own cats or cats that you know.

HAPPY COLOURING!

Remember, grooming plays a big part in building a bond between you and your cat.

Fingerprint dogs and cats.

Thumb print over corner of scrap paper and remove to leave white triangle for nose and mouth.

Stick-on eyes: Hole-punched pieces of paper with dots marked in the centres.

Or use white paint to make eyes and tummy.

There are lots of fun things on the website, including an online quiz, e-cards, colouring sheets and recipes for making dog and cat treats.

www.battersea.org.uk